刘墉

绘著

刘轩 刘倚帆 译

随遇随喜

刘墉写给大家的
生活禅

湖南文艺出版社
HUNAN LITERATURE AND ART PUBLISHING HOUSE

博集天卷
CS-BOOKY

日日是好日，时时是好时

佛教三藏经典，九千余卷，浩如烟海，为了要让大家能明白，佛陀说法度众，也常引用譬喻辅以说明，给人接受，进而在生活里实践、受用。

回想我初到台湾，为了把人间佛教带到每个地方，常常借用庙口讲演，只要我讲到故事，群众就会慢慢向我集中，故事讲完之后叙述义理，大家又慢慢散去，一场讲演大约两个小时，群众就像潮水一样来来去去，都要好几回合。

我从那里学到一个经验，人人爱听故事，有时要"以事显理"，有时要"以理明事"，理事要圆融，要契理契机，只有将故事与佛理结合，才是最好的弘法讲演。这也是我后来一直很用心佛经里的故事，或重视人间社会生活小故事的原因。

所谓"小沙弥不可轻，将来成为大法王；小儿童不可轻，将来是国家栋梁"，本书是刘墉先生结集二十篇小沙弥的故事，借由老和尚的佛法、人生经验，以简短巧妙的譬喻教导小沙弥，引导阅读者拥有正确的人生观，在面对多变的现实生活，不致迷失方向，以智慧跳脱困境，得到解脱自在。

刘墉先生兼具多种身份，他是名作家，也是画家，更是一位热心公益的文化人，他对生命的热爱，对生活的热情，从这本书可见一斑。每篇文章搭配彩色水墨画，柔和细腻的色调，加上活泼生动的布局，增强故事的张力，让阅读者多了图像的思考空间，相信大家一定会很喜爱。我非常乐见它的出版并且向大家推荐。

是为序。

星云

二〇二〇年三月 于佛光山开山寮

With the Tripitaka and more than 9,000 other volumes, Buddhist teachings are as vast as the sea. To help everybody understand, the Buddha lectured on doctrines to enlighten crowds, and he also utilized descriptive analogies, which people could accept and then practice and benefit from in everyday life.

Thinking back to when I first arrived in Taiwan, in order to bring Humanistic Buddhism to all places, I frequently lectured at temple gates. When I told stories, the crowds gradually gathered around me. When I finished the stories and spoke about theories, people gradually dispersed. Each lecture was approximately two hours, and the crowds came and went like tides, multiple times.

I learned from that experience that all people love to listen to stories. Sometimes, we need stories to demonstrate principles; other times, we need principles to explain stories. Principles and stories must round each other out, while being true both to teachings and to humans' hearts. Combining stories and principles is the only way to give the best kind of Buddhist lecture. This is why since then I have always been very attentive to the stories in the Buddhist scriptures and to the little stories in human societies and everyday lives.

We similarly say: "Don't underestimate the little monk, for he can later become the great master; don't underestimate the small child, for he can later be the beam holding up the country." This book is Mr. Yong Liu's compilation of twenty Little Monk stories. Through the old Master's Buddhist teachings and life experience, he uses simple clever analogies to teach the Little Monk. This guides readers to have a correct outlook on life and, when facing the ever-changing realities of life, to not lose one's direction but rather use wisdom to overcome obstacles and achieve the relief of freedom.

Mr. Yong Liu has many identities. He is a famous writer, and he is also an artist. He is furthermore a public-spirited man of culture. His love of life and his enthusiasm for living can be clearly seen in this book. Every story is paired with a watercolor and ink drawing, of delicate and exquisite colors and lively and vivid composition, which increases the story's tension and gives readers a visual space for imagination. I believe everyone will really enjoy this book. I am very happy to see it published, and I recommend it to all.

This is the foreword.

Hsing Yun

Fo Guang Shan Institute of Humanistic Buddhism, March 2020

刘爷爷说故事

　　我在台北跟儿子住得很近，儿子和儿媳妇一有应酬，我就去监督孙子孙女吃饭。这是我很乐意做而且引以为傲的，因为在我的监督之下，两个小鬼比他们父母在家时吃得快。我用的方法是"故事配饭"，只要我开讲，两个小鬼会瞪大眼睛听。他们不好好吃，我就不往下讲，为了继续往下听，十岁的孙女和八岁的孙子总会大口地把饭吃完。

　　我很爱写故事、说故事，会为大人写《冷眼看人生》和《我不是教你诈》，也会为青少年写《点一盏心灯》和《捕梦网》，因为我发现说故事是最好的教育方法，它不生硬、不教条，能够把很深的道理，用引人入胜的方式传达。

　　这本书里收纳了我过去五十年间写的小故事，虽然主角只有小沙弥跟老师父，但是完全没有宗教性，我只是借着一对师徒，说些人生的道理。因为文字浅、寓意深，七八岁的小孩能听得懂，七八十岁的读者也能发会心的一笑。

　　书里的插图都是我亲自绘制的，有人笑我把"画大画"的时间拿来作"小人儿书"，岂知"边写边画"是我人生最大的乐事。

　　英译由倚帆和刘轩完成，其中很多故事是他们小时候听过的，除了更能心领神会，还重温了童年往事，希望这本书也能带给更多人快乐的时光。

刘墉

二〇二〇年三月

I live very close to my son in Taipei. When my son and daughter-in-law aren't home for dinner, I go over to supervise my grandson and granddaughter as they eat. This is something I am glad to do and proud to do because, under my supervision, the two little monsters eat faster than when their parents are home. My method is "stories with rice." When I tell a story, they listen with widened eyes. If they don't eat what they should, then I stop telling the story. For me to continue the story, my 10-year-old granddaughter and 8-year-old grandson always take big bites to finish their meal.

I love to write stories and tell stories. I've written *A Hard Look at Humanity* and *I'm Not Teaching You to Be Conniving* for adults, and I've written *Light the Lamp in Your Heart* and *Dreamcatcher* for young adults. I've realized that telling stories is the best way to teach. Stories are neither rigid nor dogmatic; they can communicate profound philosophy in a fascinating manner.

This book compiles short stories that I have written over the past 50 years. Although the main characters are a Little Monk and his old Master, this book is not meant to be religious. I am merely demonstrating life philosophies through the relationship of master and apprentice. The word choice is simple, while the morals of the stories are deep. Seven- or eight-year-old children can understand, and 70- or 80-year-old readers can also knowingly smile.

I personally drew all the illustrations in this book. Some people joke that I spend time that could be spent on great paintings to instead produce a book for little ones. What they don't know is that writing and drawing at the same time is one of the greatest joys of my life.

The English translations were done by my daughter Yvonne and my son Xuan. They had heard me tell many of these stories when they were younger, and so they very well understand the unspoken meanings behind the words. These stories refresh their childhood memories, and we hope this book brings joy to more people.

Yong Liu
March 2020

随遇随喜
YIELD TO JOY

目 录
CONTENTS

放下 · 放空 · 放平 ·
放心 · 放手

To Give

随遇随喜
YIELD TO JOY

小沙弥对什么都好奇。秋天，禅院里红叶飞舞，小沙弥跑去问师父："红叶这么美，为什么会掉呢？"

师父一笑："因为冬天来了，树撑不住那么多叶子，只好舍。这不是'放弃'，是'放下'！"

Little Monk was curious about everything. In autumn, red foliage fluttered in the monastery yard. Little Monk asked Master, "These leaves are so beautiful. Why do they fall?"

Master smiled. "Winter is coming, and the tree cannot hold on to so many leaves, so it must choose. The tree is not giving up; rather, it is choosing to give away."

冬天来了，小沙弥看见师兄们把院子里的水缸扣过来，又跑去问师父："好好的水，为什么要倒掉呢？"

师父笑笑："因为冬天冷，水结冻膨胀，会把缸撑破，所以要倒干净。这不是'真空'，是'放空'！"

大雪纷飞，厚厚的，一层又一层，积在几棵盆栽的龙柏上，师父要小沙弥帮忙把盆扳倒，让树躺下来。

Winter arrived. Curious Little Monk saw elder monks turning over the water barrels one by one. He asked Master, "There is still good water in many of the barrels. Why must we pour the water out?"

Master smiled. "When the water freezes, it will crack the barrels, so we must pour all the water out. We are not depleting the barrels; rather, we are unloading them."

A blizzard came, sweeping piles of thick snow onto the junipers. Master asked Little Monk to help tip the potted saplings over.

随遇随喜
YIELD TO JOY

小沙弥又不解了，急着问："龙柏好好的，为什么弄倒？"

师父脸一整："谁说好好的？你没见雪把柏叶都压塌了吗？再压就断了。那不是'放倒'，是'放平'，为了保护它，教它躺平休息休息，等雪霁再扶起来。"

天寒，加上全球金融危机，香油收入少多了，连小沙弥都紧张，跑去问师父怎么办。

Little Monk was confused. "Aren't the saplings doing fine? Why lay them down?"

Master replied sternly: "Who says they're doing fine? Don't you see how the snow is weighing them down? By laying the saplings down, we are protecting them, so that they may stand again after the snow. We are not forcing them to fall over; rather, we are teaching them to rest."

The winter was harsh and long, and with a global recession, the monastery's offering box was running empty. Even Little Monk felt nervous and asked Master what to do.

随遇随喜
YIELD TO JOY

"少你吃，少你穿了吗？"师父瞪一眼，"数数！柜里还挂了多少衣服？柴房里还堆了多少柴？仓房里还积了多少粮食？别想没有的，想想还有的；苦日子总会过去，春天总会来到。你要放心。'放心'不是'不用心'，是把心安顿。"

"Have you been eating or wearing less?" Master replied with a glare. "Go see for yourself: How much clothing is there in the closet? How much firewood is there in the shed? How much food is there in the barn? Stop thinking about what we don't have, and think about what we do have. The hard times will pass, and spring will come. You need to trust. This does not mean you stop being mindful; rather, you calm your heart with trust."

随遇随喜
YIELD TO JOY

春天果然跟着来了，大概因为冬天的雪水特别多，春花烂漫，更胜往年，前殿的香火也渐渐恢复往日的盛况。师父要出远门了，小沙弥追到山门："师父您走了，我们怎么办？"

师父笑着挥挥手："你们能放下、放空、放平、放心，我还有什么不能放手的呢？"

Spring indeed arrived, and the thawing snow made for even more blossoms than last year. Worshippers returned, and the offering box became full again. It was then that Master prepared to set off on a long journey. Little Monk ran up to him at the mountain gate. "Master! When you are gone, what are we going to do?"

Master smiled and waved his hand. "You have already learned how to give away, to unload, to rest, and to trust. Is there any reason why I should not let go?"

放，不是放弃，不是放任，
不是放恣，不是放纵，不是放逐。

不曾拿起，怎么放下？
不曾拥有，怎么放空？
不曾独立，怎么放平？
不曾挂念，怎么放心？
不曾抓紧，怎么放手？

有收才能放，有放才能收！

Letting go is not letting alone, and it is not giving up. It does not indulge with abandon, nor does it abandon through rejection.

If you do not pick up, then how can you give away?
If you do not acquire, then how can you unload?
If you do not strive, then how can you rest?
If you do not care, then how can you trust?
If you do not hold on, then how can you let go?

Just as you need to take in order to give, you must give in order to take!

随遇随喜
YIELD TO JOY

16

天地禅院

The Temple Between Heaven and Earth

随遇随喜
YIELD TO JOY

小沙弥坐在地上哭，四周都是写了字的废纸。

"怎么啦？"师父问。

"写不好。"

师父捡起几张看："写得不错嘛，为什么要扔掉？又为什么哭？"

Little Monk sat on the floor, crying. All around were discarded papers with writing on them.

"What's the matter?" Master asked.

"I can't write well."

Master glanced at a few pages. "They are not bad! Why discard them? And why cry about it?"

"我就是觉得不好。"小沙弥继续哭，"我喜欢完美，一点都不能错。"

"问题是，这世界上有谁能一点都不错呢？"师父拍拍小沙弥，"你什么都要完美，一点不满意，就生气、就哭，这反而是不完美了。"

"I think they are no good." Little Monk sulked. "I need perfection. I can't tolerate a single mistake."

"Well, question is, can anyone in this world never make mistakes?" Master gently patted Little Monk. "You want everything to be perfect; but if dissatisfaction makes you angry and tearful, then that alone would be an imperfection."

随遇随喜
YIELD TO JOY

小沙弥把地上的纸捡起来，先去洗了手；又照照镜子，去洗脸；再把裤子脱下来，洗了一遍又一遍。

"你这是在干吗啊？你洗来洗去，已经浪费半天时间了。"师父问。

"我有洁癖！"小沙弥说，"我容不得一点脏，您没发现吗？每个施主走后，我都把他坐过的椅子擦一遍。"

Little Monk picked up the papers, washed his hands, looked in the mirror, and washed his face. He then took off his pants and washed them over and over.

"What are you doing? You're washing this and that and wasting half the day," Master said.

"I am obsessed with cleanliness!" Little Monk said. "I cannot tolerate any dirt. Haven't you noticed that after every guest leaves, I always wipe his chair clean?"

随遇随喜
YIELD TO JOY

"这叫洁癖吗？"师父笑笑，"你嫌天脏、嫌地脏、嫌人脏，外表虽然干净，内心反而有病，是不洁净了。"

"Is this so-called cleanliness obsession?" Master chuckled. "If you are always complaining that everything and everyone is dirty, then even when you look clean on the outside, your spirit is actually sick and impure on the inside."

小沙弥要去化缘，特别挑了一件破旧的衣服穿。

"为什么挑这件呢？"师父问。

"您不是说不必在乎表面吗？"小沙弥有点不服气，"所以我找件破旧的衣服。而且这样施主们才会同情，才会多给钱。"

Little Monk set out to collect alms, wearing a set of particularly shabby clothes.

"Why did you choose to wear these clothes?" Master asked.

"Didn't you teach us to look past the surface?" Little Monk said with a hint of sarcasm. "That's why I wear shabby clothes. And this way, benefactors will take pity on me and donate more."

随遇随喜
YIELD TO JOY

"你是去化缘，还是去乞讨？"师父瞪了眼睛，"你是希望人们看你可怜，施舍你？还是希望人们看你有为，透过你度化更多人？"

"Are you collecting alms, or are you begging?" Master looked stern. "Do you want people to take pity on you and treat you as charity? Or do you want people to see promise in you and aspire to higher spiritual purpose through you?"

师父圆寂了，小沙弥成为住持。

他总是穿得整整齐齐，拿着医疗箱，到最脏乱贫困的地区，为那里的病人洗脓、换药，然后脏兮兮地回山门。

Master passed away. Little Monk became the abbot.

It is said that he always dresses neatly, carrying a medical kit to the poorest slums, cleaning wounds and changing bandages for the sick before returning to the temple, soiled from head to toe.

随遇随喜
YIELD TO JOY

他也总是亲自去化缘，但是左手化来的钱，右手就济助了可怜人。他很少待在禅院，禅院也不曾扩建，但是他的信众愈来愈多，大家跟着他上山、下海，到偏远的山村和渔港。

He also personally makes the rounds to collect alms, but whatever he takes in immediately goes to help the needy. He is rarely at the temple, which hasn't expanded in years, yet his followers are always increasing in number. They follow him from mountain to sea, into remote towns and fishing villages.

"师父在世的时候，教导我什么叫完美，完美就是求这世界完美；师父也告诉我什么是洁癖，洁癖就是帮助不洁的人，使他洁净。师父还开示我，什么是化缘，化缘是使人们能彼此帮助，让众生结善缘。"新的住持说。

"至于什么是禅院，禅院不见得要在山林，而应该在人间。南北西东，皆是我弘法的所在；天地之间，就是我的禅院。"

"When my Master was alive, he taught me the meaning of perfection, which is to make this world as good as it can be. Master taught me that obsession about cleanliness should be applied to help those who are unclean become clean. Master also enlightened me on the meaning of alms, which is to enable people to help one another and to bond through good deeds," said the abbot.

"And what is a temple? A temple shouldn't be secluded in mountain forests. It should be among the people. North, south, east, west- I carry forward the teaching of the truth. And anywhere between heaven and earth, you shall find my temple."

随遇随喜
YIELD TO JOY

心上的落叶

Fallen Leaves of the Heart

深秋了，小沙弥每天忙着扫落叶，一边扫一边落，常常早晨才扫干净，下午又落满了庭院，还得再扫一次。

"哪里是落叶？根本是烦恼嘛！"小沙弥边扫边怨，正巧被师父听到了。

It was late autumn, and Little Monk was busy sweeping leaves every day. While he swept, the leaves kept falling. It often took him all morning to sweep the courtyard clean, and by the afternoon, he had to do it all over again.

"You aren't just leaves; you're trouble!" Little Monk complained as he swept, and Master overheard him.

"你说落叶是烦恼？"师父笑问，"说得好！说得好！烦恼来了，扫掉！烦恼再来，再扫掉！"

"可是风大，还会把别处的落叶吹过来。"小沙弥指着禅院的围墙说，"咱们的墙太矮，门又总是开着，外面的落叶会偷偷溜进来。"

"里面的落叶不是也会被风吹出去吗？扫落叶不必问它的来处，既然落在咱们院里，就咱们管！"

"You say the leaves are trouble?" Master asked with a smile. "Well said, well said! When trouble comes, we sweep it away! When trouble comes again, we sweep it away again!"

"The wind is too strong. It keeps bringing leaves from other places," Little Monk said and pointed at the monastery walls. "Our walls are too low, and our gates are always open. Fallen leaves find a way to sneak in."

"Well, don't some of our fallen leaves get blown out as well? There's no need to mind where the leaves come from. As long as the leaves are in our garden, we'll take care of it!"

随遇随喜
YIELD TO JOY

师父拍拍小沙弥：

"有新绿，就有枯叶；有得意，就有烦恼。今天落，今天扫；明天落，明天扫。不必因为扫了还会落，就不扫。

"我们心里也有这样的庭院，有花开就有花落，有叶生就有叶落。不怕落叶多，只要勤打扫，不疾不徐、一帚一帚，慢慢扫，扫也是一种修行。"

Master patted Little Monk gently. "Where leaves grow, leaves will fall. Where there is happiness, there is also sorrow. If the leaves fall today, then we sweep today; if the leaves fall tomorrow, then we sweep tomorrow. Although we know more leaves will fall later, we don't stop sweeping now. We have such a garden in our hearts too. Flowers bloom and wilt; leaves grow and are cast away. We do not see them as troubles, as long as we keep sweeping. Diligently, steadily, sweep by sweep—let the sweeping become your meditation."

随遇随喜
YIELD TO JOY

从我们来到这个世界的那一刻，就有了不断的相聚与别离，就有了不断的得与失。有仓廪就难免鼠患，有子女就难免烦恼，有爱情就难免牵挂，有身体就难免病痛……

From the moment we arrive in this world, people come together and separate repeatedly; we gain and lose repeatedly. If we harvest and store, then we inevitably suffer from rats. If we have sons and daughters, then we inevitably worry. If we love someone, then we inevitably care too much. If we have a body, then we inevitably fall ill.

师父的葫芦

Master's Gourd

小沙弥去见师父：

"师父！我时时打坐，常常念经，早起早睡，心无杂念，没有任何人能比我更用功了，为什么我就是无法开悟？"

师父拿出一个葫芦、一把粗盐，交给小和尚：

"去装满水，再把盐倒进去，使它溶化，你就开悟了！"

Little Monk went to see Master.

"Master! I meditate a lot. I recite my scriptures often. I keep early hours and stay mindful all the time. I'm pretty sure no one works harder than I do. Why am I still not enlightened?"

Master took out a gourd and a handful of coarse salt, and he gave these to Little Monk. "Go fill up the gourd with water and put in the salt. Make it dissolve immediately, and then you will be enlightened!"

过不多久，小沙弥跑了回来：

"葫芦口太小，我把盐倒进去，只溶化了一部分，多半沉在底下不溶化。伸进筷子又搅不动，我还是没有办法开悟。"

Shortly after, Little Monk came back. "The opening of the gourd is too small. I put the salt in, but only some of it dissolved, while the rest stays at the bottom. I tried to reach the remaining salt with a chopstick, but there's no room to stir. I am still not enlightened."

师父笑笑，拿起葫芦倒掉一些水，只摇几下，盐就溶化了。

"一天到晚用功，不留点平常心，就如同装满水的葫芦，摇不动、搅不得，怎么化盐？又怎么开悟？"

Master smiled and picked up the gourd. He poured out some water and shook it a little, and the salt dissolved immediately. "When you study all the time but don't keep a sense of balance, you are just like this gourd filled with water: nothing shakes, nothing stirs. How can anything dissolve? When there is no room in your life, how is it possible for you to be enlightened?"

心弦

Heartstrings

师父的卧榻旁总摆着一块长长的木板。

小沙弥好奇："师父，您那块木板是做什么用的？"

"那是个没有琴弦的古琴，师父的师父留下来的。"

"没有琴弦怎么弹？您为什么不装琴弦呢？"

"师父没学过，不会弹。"

"那把它放在这儿干什么？"

There has always been a long wooden board next to Master's bed.

Little Monk curiously asked, "Master, what is the board for?"

"It is an ancient lute without strings. It was left by the Master before me," Master answered.

"How do you play it without strings? Why don't you restring it?"

"I never learned how to play it."

"Then why is it still here?"

"但识琴中趣，何劳弦上声？手不会弹，心可以弹啊！师父每次看到它，就会想：我心里的琴弦调音了吗？那音准不准？我的心里有旋律吗？那旋律美不美？"

"Without making a sound, one can still feel the joy of playing, no? Even if you cannot play it with hands, you can still play it with heart! Every time I see it, I ask myself: Have I tuned the strings in my heart? Is the tone true? Can I hear the melody in my heart? Is the melody beautiful?"

师父摩挲着古琴说："每个人的身体都是琴台，心里都有琴弦，要常常调音，声音才正；要常常拨动，才不致像块死木头。世间人的烦恼，常因为心里的音乱了。做老师的人必须时时反省，先把自己心里的琴弦调好，才能为学生调音啊！"

Master gently stroked the lute and said, "The human body is like a lute. There are strings in everyone's heart. We need to keep it in tune, so that our tone stays true; we need to keep strumming, to keep the song alive. Our worries are often due to dissonance in the heart. Those who teach must be diligent in reflection to keep their heartstrings in tune, so that we may help to tune others!"

正字与反字

The Word
and the Backward

随遇随喜
YIELD TO JOY

小沙弥满怀疑惑地去见师父：

"师父！您说好人坏人都可以度化，问题是坏人已经失去了人的本质，怎么算是人呢？既然不是人，就不应该度化他。"

师父没有立刻回答，只是拿起笔在纸上写了个"我"，但字是反写的，如同印章上的文字，左右颠倒。

The puzzled Little Monk went to see Master.

"Master, you said that everyone can become enlightened. But if a person is evil and has already lost his human nature, can he still be enlightened as a human being? I have my doubts!"

Master did not reply right away. Instead, he picked up the brush and wrote the character that means "self," except the word is flipped horizontally, as it would appear if carved on a stamp.

"这是什么？"师父问。

"这是个字。"小和尚说，"但是写反了！"

"什么字呢？"

"'我'字！"

"写反了的'我'字算不算字？"师父追问。

"不算！"

"既然不算，你为什么说它是个'我'字？"

"So, what is this?" Master asked.

"It's a word," Little Monk answered, "but backward!"

"What word is it?"

"Self!"

"Do you think this backward 'self' is still a word?" Master asked.

"No!"

"If you say it is not, then why do you still recognize it as 'self'?"

随遇随喜
YIELD TO JOY

"算！"小沙弥立刻改口。

"既算是个字，你为什么说它反了呢？"

小和尚怔住了，不知怎样作答。

"Um...yes, it is a word then!" Little Monk corrected himself immediately.

"If it's a word, then why do you say it's backward?"

Little Monk did not know what to say.

"正字是字，反字也是字，你说它是'我'字，又认得出那是反字，主要是因为你心里认得真正的'我'字；相反地，如果你原先不识字，就算我写反了，你也分不出来，只怕当人告诉你那是个'我'字之后，遇到正写的'我'字，你倒要说是写反了！"师父说。

"A word is a word, even when backward. You recognize this 'self' as backward because you have an impression of a correct 'self' in your heart. On the other hand, if you were illiterate, it would make no difference if I wrote it one way or another. In fact, if you learned it this way, one day when you see the right word, you may very well claim that it's backward!" Master said.

随遇随喜
YIELD TO JOY

"同样的道理，好人是人，坏人也是人，最重要的是你要认得人的本性，于是当你遇到恶人的时候，仍然一眼便能见到他的'天质'，并唤出他的'本真'。本真显现，就不难度化了！"

"This principle also applies to people. Whether good people or bad people, they are all people. The most important thing is to recognize their humanity. Therefore, when you meet sinful people, you can see through to their human character and call out to their authentic humanity. When their authenticity is made obvious, enlightenment is made possible!"

好好活着

Live Well

大热天，禅院里的花被晒蔫了。

"天哪，快浇点水吧！"小沙弥喊着，接着去提了桶水来。

"别急！"师父说，"现在太阳大，一冷一热，非死不可，等晚一点再浇。"

傍晚，那盆花已经成了"梅干菜"的样子。

On a hot day, the flowers in the monastery were withering under the sun.

"My goodness! Let's hurry and water them!" shouted Little Monk, as he carried over a bucket of water.

"Don't rush!" said Master. "The sun is too strong now. Being cold in one minute and hot in another will make them die for sure. Wait until it's cooler outside to water them."

By that evening, the flowers had already looked like dried pickled vegetables.

小沙弥咕咕哝哝地说："一定已经死透了，怎么浇也活不了了。"

"少啰唆！浇！"师父骂。

水浇下去，没多久，已经垂下去的花，居然全站了起来，而且生意盎然。

"天哪！"小沙弥喊，"它们可真厉害，憋在那儿，撑着不死。"

"胡说！"师父骂，"不是撑着不死，是好好活着。"

Little Monk muttered, "They must be completely dead by now. No amount of water can save them."

"Stop muttering! Water!" Master scolded.

Soon after watering, the previously drooping flowers surprisingly all perked up and looked full of life.

"My goodness!" Little Monk shouted. "They are truly impressive. They held on and resisted death."

"Nonsense!" Master scolded. "They were not resisting death; they were living well."

随遇随喜
YIELD TO JOY

"这有什么不同呢？"小和尚低着头。

"当然不同。"师父拍拍小和尚，"我问你，我今年八十多了，我是撑着不死，还是好好活着？"

晚课完了，师父把小和尚叫到面前问："怎么样？想通了吗？"

"没有。"小沙弥还低着头。

师父敲了小和尚一下。

"What is the difference?" asked Little Monk with his head down.

"Of course there is a difference." Master patted Little Monk. "Let me ask you: I am over 80 years old this year. Am I resisting death, or am I living well?"

After Night Prayer, Master called Little Monk over and asked, "How do you feel? Have you figured it out?"

"No," said Little Monk, still with his head down.

Master knocked Little Monk on the head.

随遇随喜
YIELD TO JOY

"笨哪！一天到晚怕死的人，是撑着不死；每天都向前看的人，是好好活着。得一天寿命，就要好好过一天。那些活着的时候天天为了怕死而拜佛烧香，希望死后能成佛的，绝对成不了佛。"师父说，"他今生能好好过，都没好好过，老天何必给他死后更好的日子？"

"Silly! Someone who is afraid of death from morning to night is resisting death. Someone who looks to the future every day is living well. When you are blessed with another day of life, you should live well for another day. Some people always pray and burn incense because they are afraid of death and hope to achieve Buddhahood after death; they will certainly not achieve Buddhahood."

Master continued: "If a person who is able to live well in this life never lives well, then why would the heavens give him a better life after death?"

杀手的爱

A Killer's Love

随遇随喜

YIELD TO JOY

小沙弥正在练字，突然听见窗外传来"啪"的一声，抬头看，是只大螳螂落在纱窗上。

小沙弥兴奋地走到窗前，贴近看。

突然"啪"的一声，又飞来一只螳螂，居然以迅雷不及掩耳的速度，爬到先前螳螂的背上。

"专心写字，不要看！"师父说，"深秋了，到它们交配的季节了。"

Little Monk was practicing his writing when he heard a sudden "pa" sound from outside of the window. He looked up and saw a large praying mantis had landed on the window screen.

Little Monk excitedly walked to the window to take a closer look.

Suddenly there was another "pa"! A second praying mantis had flown over, and with lightning speed, it climbed onto the first praying mantis' back.

"Focus on your writing! Don't look!" said Master. "It's late autumn now, which is their mating season."

小沙弥定睛，果然两只螳螂屁股连在一块儿，小沙弥有点不好意思，回到桌上写字，但是一边写一边偷偷看。

"不得了了！师父！"小沙弥突然放下笔喊，"它们在打架，一只咬另一只，那只居然不躲，头都被咬掉了！"

"专心写字！"师父没抬头，"它愿意被咬，就让它咬吧！"

Little Monk stared. The two praying mantises' butts were sure enough connected. Little Monk felt a bit shy. He went back to his desk, but he continued to peek at the window while writing.

"Oh no! Master!" Little Monk suddenly shouted as he put down his pen. "They're fighting! One is biting the other, and the one being bitten isn't even running away. His head is nearly bitten off!"

"Focus on your writing!" said Master without looking up. "One is willing to be bitten, so let the other one bite!"

随遇随喜
YIELD TO JOY

"一只欺侮一只怎么成呢？"小沙弥嘟着嘴喊，"还在咬！后来的那只已经被吃掉一半了！它怎么不躲呢？它疼不疼？"

"一个愿吃，一个愿挨。有它们的道理，不用管！"

天渐黑，两只螳螂只剩一只了，凶悍的那一只因为吃了别人，肚子变得好大。

"How can one bully the other?" Little Monk shouted with a pouty face. "It's still biting! That second praying mantis only has half his body left! Why doesn't he run away? Does he feel pain?"

"One wants to eat, and the other wants to suffer. They have their reasons. Don't mind them!"

As the sky darkened, only one of the two praying mantises remained. The aggressive one's belly was big from eating the other one.

随遇随喜
YIELD TO JOY

小沙弥有点伤心，对师父说："不是不能杀生吗？人不杀，野兽就可以吃野兽，虫子就能吃虫子吗？它们的吃，不是杀生吗？"

"它们的杀，是为了生。不杀就不能生。"师父也走到窗边，看那只大肚子的螳螂，"它们是一公一母，被吃掉的是公的。"

Little Monk felt a bit sad. He said to Master:"Isn't it wrong to kill? Humans should not kill, but it's okay for animals to eat animals, and insects to eat insects? Isn't their eating a type of killing?"

"Their killing is for the purpose of living. If they don't kill, then they cannot live." Master also walked to the window and looked at the praying mantis with the big belly. "They were one male and one female. The one who was eaten was male."

小沙弥大吃一惊："那它们就是夫妻了，不是太太把先生吃了吗？这真是太狠毒了！天理难容啊！"

师父笑笑："母螳螂吃公螳螂也是天理，你以后就懂了！"

隔天清早，小沙弥急着跑到窗边看。

"母螳螂不见了！"小沙弥喊。

Little Monk was shocked. "That means they were husband and wife! The wife ate her husband? That is truly brutal! That goes against natural principles!"

Master smiled. "Female praying mantises eating male praying mantises is an act of natural principle. You'll understand later!"

Early the next morning, Little Monk hurried to look out the window.

"The female praying mantis is gone!" Little Monk hollered.

随遇随喜
YIELD TO JOY

"应该是去下蛋了！"师父说。

"下蛋？"小沙弥瞪大了眼睛。

"是啊！天就要冷了，螳螂受不了，在被冻死之前，它会先下蛋，蛋不怕寒，隔年天暖就会跑出好多螳螂宝宝。"

"可……可是那太太又为什么把丈夫吃掉呢？"

"She probably left to lay eggs!" said Master.

"To lay eggs?" Little Monk widened his eyes in disbelief.

"Yes! The days are getting colder, and the praying mantis cannot survive for much longer. Before freezing to death, she lays eggs. The eggs are not afraid of frost. When the weather turns warm next year, many baby praying mantises will emerge."

"But... But why did the wife eat the husband?"

"是公螳螂自愿的，你没看到它都不躲吗？"

师父说："你想想，秋天了，连蜜蜂蚂蚁都要冬眠了，螳螂已经不容易找到食物，母螳螂交配之后要下蛋，好比孕妇需要进补，问题是哪儿来营养呢？为了让下一代能够延续，公螳螂就奉献了自己。

"The male praying mantis was willingly eaten. Didn't you see he did not run away?"

Master turned around to face Little Monk. "Think about it. It's autumn. Even the bees and ants will soon hibernate. Praying mantises cannot easily find food. The female must lay eggs after mating, and just like a pregnant woman, she needs nutrition. The problem is: where can she get nutrition? For the sake of the next generation, the male sacrificed himself.

随遇随喜
YIELD TO JOY

"所以世间万物，不能只从表面看，也不能随便论断。千年亿载、斗转星移，能够繁衍到今天的万物，或是弱肉强食，或是牺牲奉献，即使'杀'也可能隐藏了'生'的道理。"

That is why for all the living beings on this earth, you cannot simply look at the surface or quickly judge them. Over hundreds of millions of years, the living beings that still live today have survived by being the strongest or by learning to sacrifice. Even in 'killing,' there are big hidden principles of 'living.'"

自损

Cutting Losses

刮台风，禅院里的一棵大树倒了，小沙弥惊慌地向师父报告。

"只是倒了，根还在。"师父说，"扶起来就好！"

小沙弥说："我们扶了，树太重，扶不动耶！"

"给它减重啊！"师父说，"把枝子锯掉！"

"把枝子锯掉？"小沙弥瞪大眼睛喊，"大树已经够可怜了！为什么还要伤害它？"

After a typhoon, a big tree in the monastery courtyard fell. Little Monk ran to Master in a panic.

Master said, "The tree has fallen, but its roots are intact. You can set it right!"

"We've tried, but it's too heavy!" Little Monk said.

"Then saw off some branches to lighten the load!" Master said.

"Saw off some branches?" Little Monk shouted with widened eyes. "But the tree is already damaged. Why must we hurt it more?"

"倒下的树不减重，怎么扶？失败的人还死要面子，怎么东山再起？"

"把枝子先锯掉一些，免得再被吹倒。"师父下令，"树大招风，先自损，才能不受损。"

树被锯得只剩几根大枝子，光秃秃地被扶正，怎么看怎么不顺眼，但是才不久，秃枝上就冒出新绿，隔年居然长得跟原先一样繁茂了。

"If a fallen tree does not cut its losses, then it cannot be set right. Similarly, if a fallen man does not set aside his ego, then he cannot make things right."

"Saw off some branches before the next typhoon," Master commanded. "Sometimes, we need to cut our losses before our losses catch up to us."

And so, the tree was set upright, with only a few branches remaining. It certainly looked odd. But before long, new leaves started to grow. A year later, the tree looked as good as the others.

随遇随喜
YIELD TO JOY

走进阳光

Walk into the Sunlight

随遇随喜
YIELD TO JOY

小沙弥跟师父坐车出去，天气很不稳定。

小沙弥怨："一下出太阳，一下阴天。"

Little Monk and Master went out in a car. The weather was quite unstable.

Little Monk complained, "It's sunny for a minute and then cloudy again!"

师父说："不！应该说是我们一下子开进阳光里，一下子又开出来了。太阳哪天会不出来呢？白天就算刮风下雨，它也躲在云层后面。所以有什么不如意，都可以看看天，告诉自己其实太阳等在那儿，就算不照过来，自己也能走进去。走进阳光里！"

Master said, "No! We should say that we are the ones who drove into the sunlight and then drove out of it. Is there ever a day when the sun does not come out? Even when there is wind and rain, the sun is hiding behind the clouds. Therefore, when things don't go your way and you feel like you're having a bad day, you can always look at the sky. Tell yourself: The sun is waiting there. Even if the sun is not shining on you, you can walk into it. Walk into the sunlight!"

随遇随喜
YIELD TO JOY

放下烦恼

Put Down the Distress

小沙弥跟师父晚上出去，山路黑，师父突然被绊了一下，向前扑倒在地上。所幸师父反应快，除了衣服沾了些尘土，没受伤。

小沙弥把师父扶起来，继续走。

"别急！先回头看看是什么东西把我绊倒？"师父说。

Little Monk and Master went out at night. The mountain roads were dark. Master suddenly tripped and fell forward. Luckily, he reacted very quickly. Besides getting some dirt on his clothes, he was not hurt.

Little Monk helped Master to stand up, and then he continued walking.

"Don't rush! First look back and see what tripped me," Master said.

小沙弥回头找，原来是块大石头。

"去你的！"小沙弥狠狠把石头踢开。

"你把石头踢到哪儿去了？石头又没错，是我自己走路不小心，你何必生它的气呢？"师父问，"而且你随便踢开，会不会把别人绊倒？"

Little Monk looked behind them. It was a large rock.

"Go away!" Little Monk said, as he harshly kicked the rock away.

"Where did you kick the rock to? The rock did not do anything wrong. I was the one who wasn't careful while walking. Why are you angry at the rock?" Master asked. "Besides, by kicking it away randomly, what if you cause someone else to trip?"

随遇随喜
YIELD TO JOY

"我生气！"小沙弥喊，"您怎么不问我疼不疼呢？刚才我踢那一下，脚好疼啊！"

"你有知，它无知，你跟它生气，能不吃亏吗？"师父说，"你可以把石头移开，放到它应该在的地方，譬如它是从挡土墙上掉下来的，就放回挡土墙，让它继续担任挡土的工作。

"I'm angry!" Little Monk shouted. "Why don't you ask if I got hurt? My foot hurts so much from that kick!"

"You have feelings; it does not. If you get angry at it, then of course you would be at a disadvantage," Master said. "You can move the rock away and place it where it should be. For example, if it fell out of the retaining wall, then place it back on the wall, and let it continue its job of retaining soil.

随遇随喜
YIELD TO JOY

78

"如果是从山上滚下来的，就把它安置在山边，让它别再挡路，也别再滚动。想想！刚才你那一脚，如果把石头踢到山下，会不会砸到人？如果把它踢到山坡上，它会不会继续往下滚？"

"师父说那么多，我不懂！"小沙弥嘟哝。

If it rolled down from the mountain, then place it at the side of the mountain, so that it neither blocks the road nor continues rolling. Think! If the rock fell down the mountain because of your kick, might it hit somebody? If you kicked it onto the slope, wouldn't it continue rolling?"

"Master said so much. I don't understand!" Little Monk pouted.

随遇随喜
YIELD TO JOY

师父笑笑："碰到任何烦恼，先别生气，也别把烦恼扔给别人，你要做的是先看清楚，然后心平气和地把烦恼拿起来，放到不再烦恼的地方。"

Master smiled. "When encountering distress, do not be angry in the first place, and do not transfer your distress to other people. What you must do is to first see clearly and then to calmly pick up the distress. Move it to a place where it will no longer be distressful."

接地气

Down to Earth

暮冬，冰雪刚融，禅院的围墙边就冒出好多绿色的小叶子，过几天，小叶子中间居然伸出花蕾，绽放了一朵朵小黄花、小红花、小紫花。

小沙弥蹲在花圃前，很有感触地说："这些花好小，好漂亮！可是冬天还没过，她们那么娇嫩，怎受得了呢？"

These were the last days of winter, and the land was thawing. Little green leaves had sprouted along the outer walls of the monastery. A few days later, buds appeared within the leaves, blooming into yellow, red, and purple flowers.

Little Monk crouched in front of the flowers. "The flowers look so pretty, yet so fragile! There are still some cold days ahead. How will they survive?" he asked, feeling wistful for the flowers.

师父说："她们娇嫩吗？那是番红花，别的植物连新芽都没发出来，辛夷和樱花也还在睡觉，这些小花却已经探出头了，那可不是一天两天的工夫，这表示下雪结冰的时候，她们已经在地底下一点一点往上钻。大家还在冬眠的时候，她们已经寻求突破。"

"可不是吗？"小沙弥喊着，"为什么她们比大树还厉害？"

Master said, "Do you think they are fragile? These are saffron flowers, quite different from others. While the magnolia and cherry blossoms are still asleep, these saffron flowers are awake. Under the snow and ice, they inch along day by day, so they are usually the first to break through the winter frost, before the others."

Little Monk was amazed. "Master, tell me about it. These flowers are tougher than the trees? How?"

随遇随喜
YIELD TO JOY

"因为她们藏在泥土深处啊！天没暖，大地先暖。愈接地气，愈耐寒，也愈有力量。"

"Because they stay close to the ground! The land is the first to know the changing of the seasons. The more down to earth you are, the tougher you are, and the more powerful you can be."

胜天与顺天

Conquering and Following

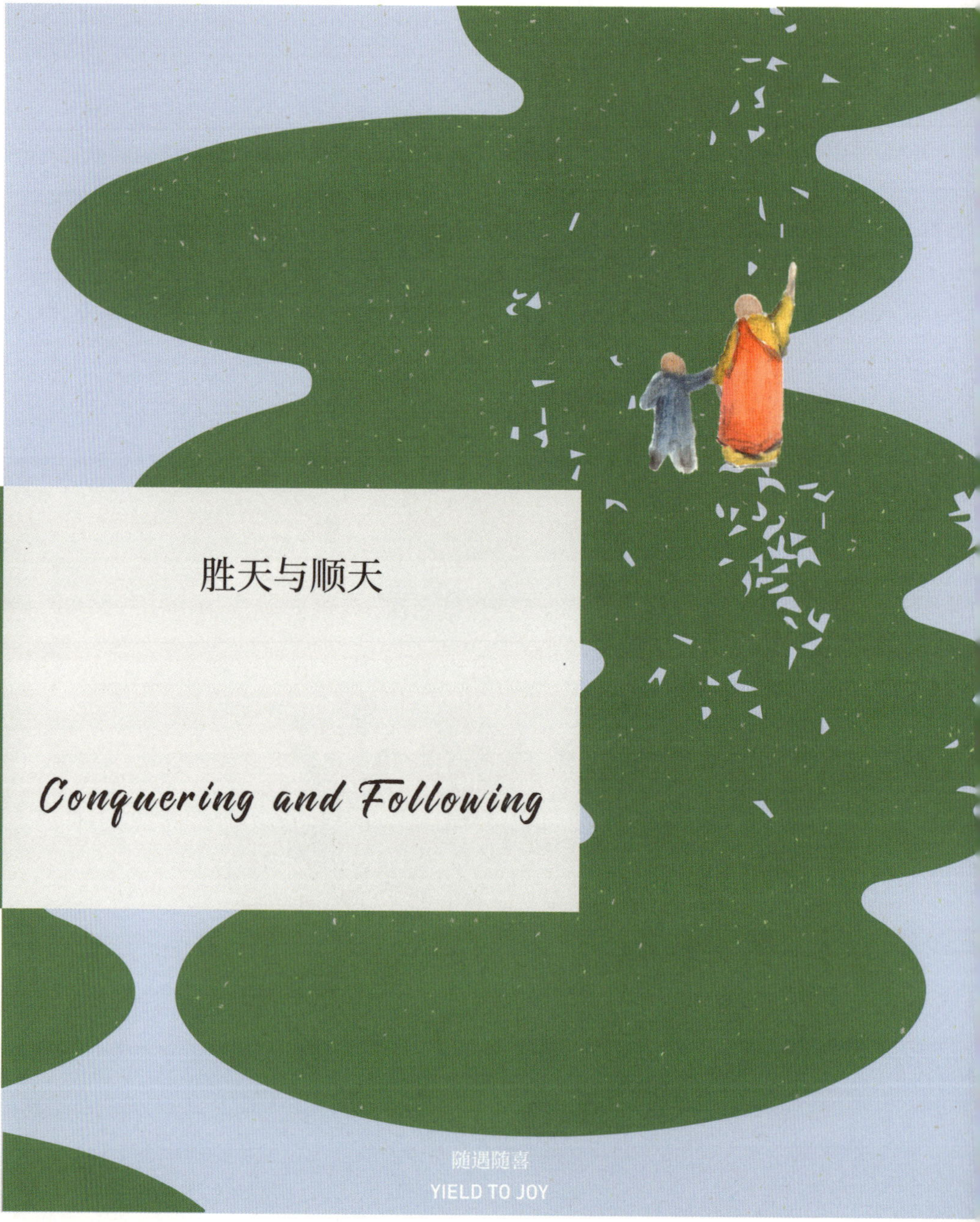

随遇随喜
YIELD TO JOY

夜里先是雷电交加，接着下起倾盆大雨，雨水像泼似的，禅院瞬间变成小池塘。

小沙弥急着把门关紧。

"别急着关门！先去检查下水道，是不是被堵住了？"师父说。

小沙弥赶紧去拿伞。

The night began with thunder and lightning, then pouring rain. Water seemed to splash from the sky, and the monastery quickly turned into a small pond.

Little Monk hurriedly closed the doors shut.

"Don't rush to close the doors! First, check the drainage system. Did it get clogged?" Master said.

Little Monk hurried to get an umbrella.

"别打伞了！雨太大，打伞也没用，还累赘。"师父说。

小沙弥冲进雨里，一下子就回来了，边跑边喊："没堵！水不但下不去，还往外冒呢——"

话没说完，突然"砰"一声，禅院的后门被撞开了，山洪像条河似的冲进来，眼看就要淹进禅房，小沙弥拿着扫把拼命往外扫，却见师父光着膀子跑向前院，把大门打开。

"Don't use an umbrella! The rain is too heavy. An umbrella would not work but would rather burden you," Master said.

Little Monk rushed into the rain and came back quickly. He shouted while running: "It's not clogged! Water is not going down, but water is coming out!" Before he could finish speaking, suddenly with a loud boom, the monastery's back door was smashed open. Water rushed in like a river and seemed close to flooding the inner rooms. Little Monk used a broom to sweep water outward with all his might, and he saw Master running toward the front door with bare arms. Master opened the front door.

随遇随喜
YIELD TO JOY

奇迹出现了！后门进来的水，原本在院子里愈积愈深，全由前门流了出去。

过不久，雨停了，小沙弥四处检查，居然没什么损失，兴奋地喊："师父好神哟！"

It was a miracle! Water that came in through the back door was previously building up inside, but now all the water flowed out through the front door.

Soon after, the rain stopped. Little Monk checked everywhere and saw that there was not much damage. He shouted excitedly, "Master is amazing!"

"关门不管用，就把门打开。雨伞挡不住，就淋着出去。"师父笑笑，"水怎么流进来，怎么流出去。不能胜天，就顺天！"

"If closing the door does not help, then open the door. If an umbrella cannot block the rain, then go outside without one," Master said with a smile. "Whichever way the water flows in, it will flow out the same way. When you cannot conquer fate, you can follow fate!"

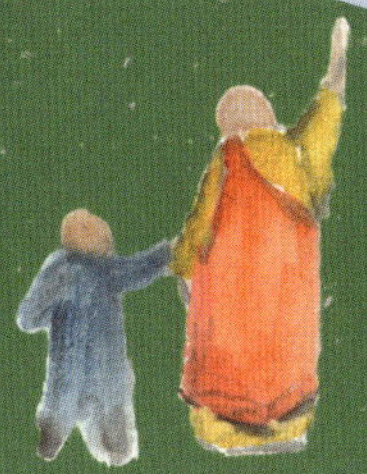

黑钵的启示

Revelation of the Black Bowl

随遇随喜
YIELD TO JOY

师父交给小沙弥一个木头做的钵："去！到溪边盛一钵水回来，要满满一钵哟！小心走，别让水溢出来。"

小沙弥出禅院、过田埂、下山坡，到小溪里舀了满满一钵水，再往回走。

Master gave Little Monk a bowl made of wood and said, "Go! Bring back a bowl of water from the creek. Make sure it is filled to the brim! Walk carefully, and don't let the water spill."

Little Monk walked out of the monastery, across the farmland, down the hill, and to the creek. He filled the bowl with water and walked back.

小沙弥边走边抱怨："院子里有方便的井水为什么不用？非要跑那么远去舀溪水？"

大概因为不专心，在好几个上坡拐弯的地方，让水溢了出去。拿给师父的时候，只剩半钵了。

隔天，师父又叫小沙弥去溪边舀水，但是把木钵换成了瓷钵。小沙弥捧着瓷钵，到溪边舀了满满一钵水，小心翼翼地走回禅房，只在爬坡时溢出一点点，得意地把接近满钵水捧给师父。

As he walked, he complained to himself: "Why couldn't I use the well that's conveniently in the monastery yard? Why did I have to come all this way to get creek water?" Perhaps because he was not paying attention, water spilled out on every uphill turn. By the time he saw Master, there was only half a bowl of water left.

The next day, Master again told Little Monk to get water from the creek, but with a porcelain bowl instead of the wooden bowl. Little Monk went to the creek and filled the porcelain bowl with water, and then he very carefully walked back, only spilling a tiny bit when climbing uphill. He proudly gave the nearly full bowl back to Master.

随遇随喜
YIELD TO JOY

第三天，师父不知从哪里掏出个黑黑脏脏的钵交给了小沙弥。

"拿这个脏东西盛水？"小沙弥问。

"嫌脏，就先洗干净。"师父说。

小沙弥用两根手指捏着那个脏钵，心想："脏死了！带臭味，还那么重，不知以前盛什么脏东西？师父有干净的钵不用，不是存心折磨我吗？"

On the third day, Master took out a bowl that was so dirty it was black, and he gave it to Little Monk.

"We're using this dirty thing for water?" Little Monk asked.

"If you think it's too dirty, then wash it first," Master answered.

Little Monk held the dirty bowl with just two fingers and thought, "It's gross! It's smelly and heavy. Who knows what it was previously used for? Master has cleaner bowls that he's not using. Is he purposely tormenting me?"

随遇随喜
YIELD TO JOY

小沙弥没好气地把那黑钵在溪水里涮了涮，又用手指搓了搓，突然眼睛一亮，钵底露出一片白，不！是一片金！

小沙弥举着钵，上气不接下气地跑回禅院，大喊着："师父，这钵是金的耶！"

师父没什么表情，沉声问："水呢？"

Little Monk annoyedly rinsed the black bowl in the creek and rubbed it with his fingers. Suddenly, his eyes lit up. There was a flash of white at the bottom of the bowl. No, it was gold!

Little Monk raised up the bowl and ran back to the monastery as fast as he could. He shouted, "Master, this bowl is made of gold!"

Master was expressionless. He asked in a low voice, "Where's the water?"

小沙弥一愣："我急着告诉您这个好消息，所以忘记舀水了！真要用金钵舀水吗？"

Little Monk was stunned. "I was in such a hurry to tell you this good news that I forgot to scoop water! Are we really using this gold bowl to scoop water?"

"金钵舀出的水，跟木钵会有差异吗？对你来说那是个贵重的金钵，对我来说只是个钵。无论木头的、白瓷的、纯金的，钵就是钵！"师父说，"如同我们度化人，要平等对待，不能因为世俗的尊卑贵贱而有差异。每个人都是会学习、能领悟的人，如同可以盛东西的钵，最重要的是我们要醍醐灌顶，敬谨小心地为他们注满。"

"Is there a difference between water scooped by a gold bowl versus a wooden bowl? You seem to say that it is a valuable gold bowl, but to me, it is simply a bowl. Whether it is made of wood, porcelain, or pure gold, a bowl is a bowl!" said Master. "Similarly, when we enlighten people, we must treat all of them equally, with no regard for secular notions of wealth or status. Every person can learn and comprehend. The most important thing is to carefully fill each person to the brim with enlightenment, just like a bowl."

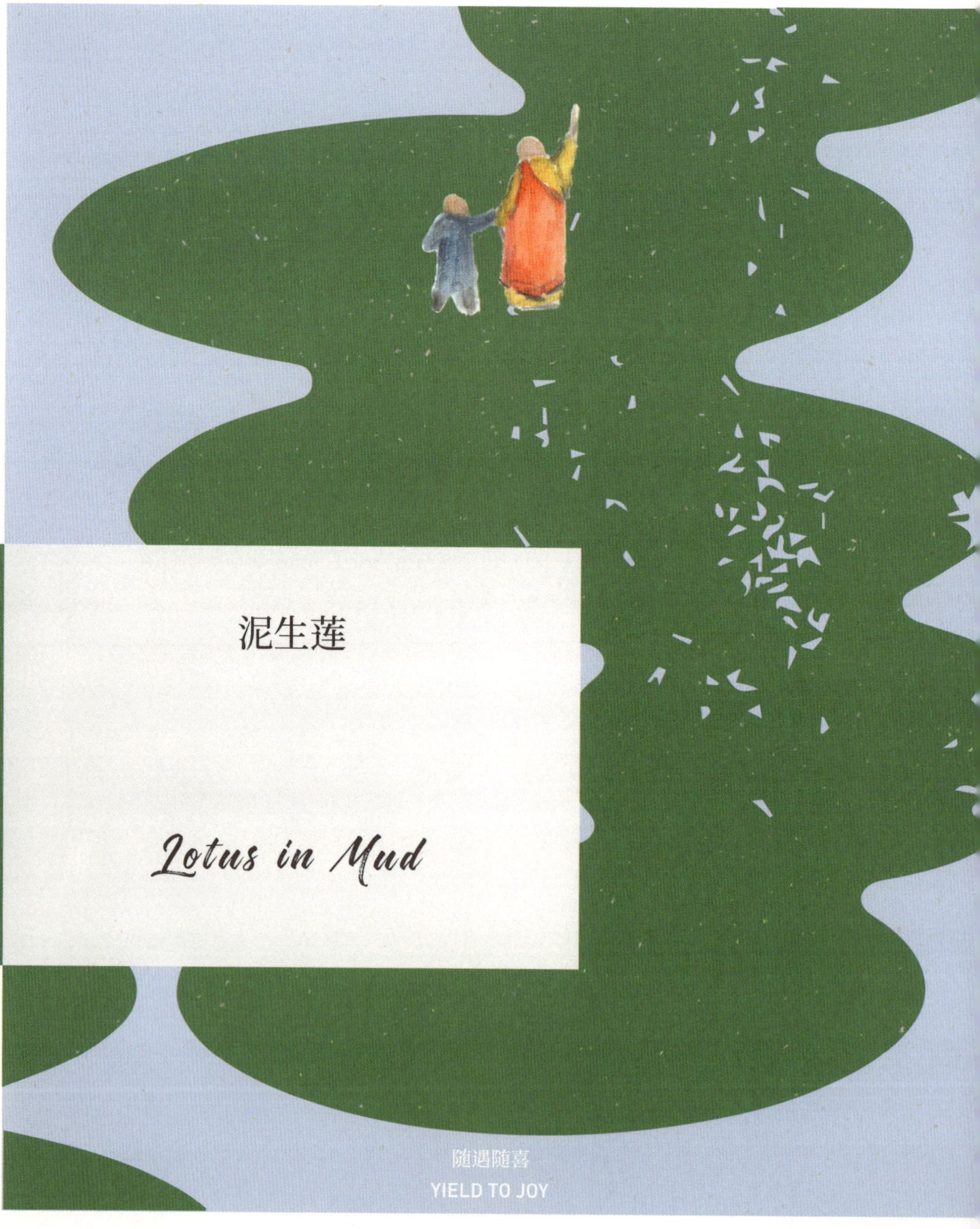

泥生莲

Lotus in Mud

随遇随喜

YIELD TO JOY

小沙弥跟师父进城，从大路进，绕小路回来。

"为什么走小路呢？旁边都是违建，好脏好臭。"小沙弥问。

师父没答话，继续走，经过一片池塘，野生的莲花正盛开着。

Little Monk and Master went into the city. They took the main road going there, but they took small side roads coming back.

"Why are we taking the side roads? There are illegal shelters here that are dirty and smelly," Little Monk asked.

Master did not answer. He continued to walk, and they passed a pond. Wild lotuses were in full bloom.

师父拍拍小沙弥："去为师父摘一朵吧！"

小沙弥二话不说就脱掉鞋子和外裤跳进池塘，只是才走两步就喊："下面都是稀泥耶，好黏啊！把我的脚都吸住了！"

"你要摘莲花就别怕稀泥！一步步走稳，稀泥不会把你吃了！"

Master nudged Little Monk and said, "Pick a flower for Master!"

Little Monk did not hesitate to take off his shoes and pants to jump into the pond. But only two steps in, he hollered, "It's all slimy mud down here! So sticky! My feet are getting stuck."

"If you want to get a lotus flower, then don't be afraid of mud! Walk steadily, one foot at a time. The mud won't eat you!"

随遇随喜
YIELD TO JOY

小沙弥终于摘到莲花，兴奋地回到岸上递给师父。"好香啊！好美啊！"小沙弥喊，可是跟着低头又哇哇叫，"我脚上都是稀泥，好脏啊！"

Little Monk finally got a lotus flower, and he excitedly returned to the shore to give the flower to Master. "It's fragrant! It's beautiful!" he exclaimed, but then he looked down and whined, "My feet are covered in slimy mud. So dirty!"

"洗洗就不脏了！"师父说，"不怕脏，怕你嫌脏的一颗心。我们度化人，经常是脚下踩着污泥，手上捧着莲花。如果你嫌脏，不愿涉过泥塘，还能摘到这朵莲花吗？如果你嫌那些小路既脏又窄，就不进去，还能发现贫民的疾苦、帮助苦难的人们吗？"

"Your feet will be clean again after a quick wash!" Master said. "Don't fear dirtiness. Fear your heart for its disgust toward dirtiness. When we enlighten people, we often have our feet stepping in mud and our hands holding a lotus flower. If you had felt disgusted and refused to cross the muddy pond, then could you have gotten this flower? If you feel disgusted toward narrow and dirty roads, and so you don't take them, then how can you discover the suffering of the poor and truly help the people?"

满了吗?

Is It Full?

随遇随喜
YIELD TO JOY

小沙弥去见师父："我已经学够了，好像可以出师了吧！"

"什么是够了呢？"师父问。

"就是满了，装不下了。"

"那么装一大碗石子来吧！"

徒弟照做了。

Little Monk went to see Master and said, "I have learned enough. I think I can graduate now!"

Master asked, "What does 'enough' mean?"

"It means something is full, and you cannot put more things in."

"Then please bring over a full bowl of stones."

The apprentice did as he was told.

"满了吗？" 师父问。

"满了！"

师父抓来一把沙，掺入碗里，没有溢。

"满了吗？" 师父又问。

"满了！"

师父抓起一把石灰，掺入碗里，还没有溢。

"满了吗？" 师父再问。

"Is it full?" Master asked.

"It's full!"

Master grabbed a handful of sand and poured it into the bowl. The bowl did not overflow.

"Is it full?" Master asked again.

"It's full!"

Master picked up a handful of garden lime and poured it into the bowl. The bowl still did not overflow.

"Is it full?" Master asked yet again.

随遇随喜
YIELD TO JOY

"满了！"

师父又倒了一盅水下去，仍然没有溢出来。

"满了吗？"

"……"

"It's full!"

Master then poured a cup of water into the bowl, and still, it did not overflow.

"Is it full?"

"…"

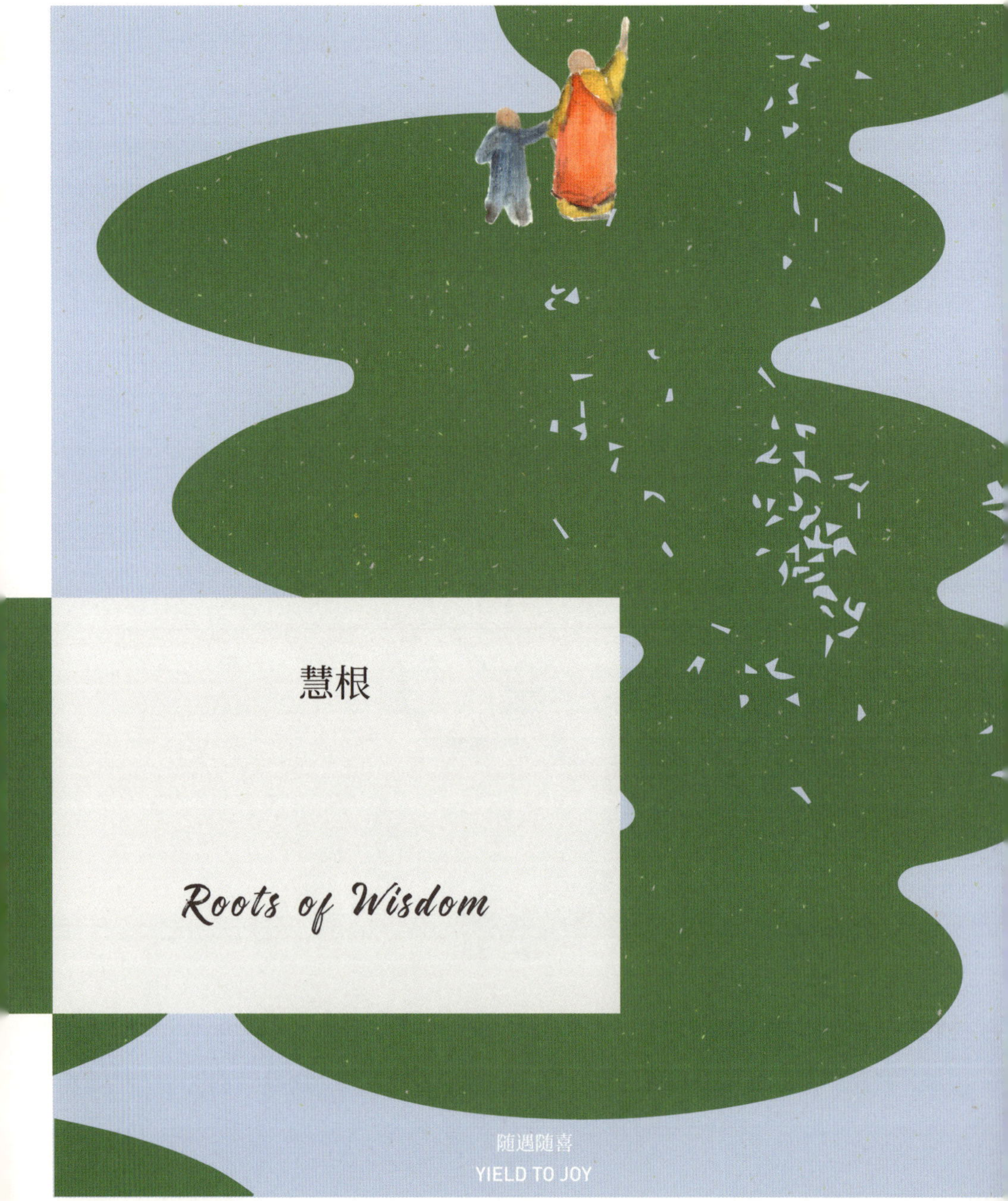

慧根

Roots of Wisdom

随遇随喜
YIELD TO JOY

过年，有信众送来一大把晚香玉。

"拿花瓶盛水，插上，这是'岁朝清供'。"师父对小沙弥说。

过了几天。

"给花换水了吗？"师父问。

小沙弥摇摇头："要换水吗？大殿里的富贵竹，插两年了，不是只要加水，不必换水吗？"

To celebrate the New Year, a believer gave the monastery a bouquet of tuberoses.

"Fill a vase with water and put the flowers in there. These are special New Year's flowers," said Master to Little Monk.

A few days passed.

"Did you change the water in the flowers' vase?" Master asked.

Little Monk shook his head. "We have to change the water? The lucky bamboo in the hall has been there for two years. I thought we only added water and never changed water?"

"富贵竹是富贵竹，它的水不会臭。"师父说，"晚香玉是晚香玉，花虽然香，水却会臭，不信你闻闻。"

小沙弥把瓶里的水倒出来。"真的臭了！"小沙弥直皱眉，"为什么它们不一样呢？"

"因为一个能生根，一个不能生根。你看富贵竹下头是不是长了好多根？再看看晚香玉，是不是不但没长根，而且烂了？"

"Bamboo is bamboo. Its water will not stink," said Master. "Tuberoses are tuberoses. Although the flowers smell nice, the water eventually stinks. Take a sniff if you don't believe me."

Little Monk poured the water out of the vase. "It really does stink!" Little Monk said with a frown. "Why aren't all plants the same?"

"One can grow roots, while the other cannot. Do you see the many roots growing out from the bottom of the lucky bamboo? Now look at the tuberoses. They not only don't have roots growing out, but rather they're rotting at the bottom, right?"

随遇随喜
YIELD TO JOY

师父拍拍小沙弥："生根，是活的；不生根，是死的。"

夏天，午后总有雷雨。

禅房的一侧地势低，一下大雨就积水。

"把下面的墙板换换吧！"师父指示小沙弥，"泡太久，都朽了！"

果然靠地面的墙板，全一扯就下来了。师父抱来新的木板，两个人一起钉上。

Master patted Little Monk and continued, "Something that takes root is alive. Something that does not take root is dead."

That summer, there were often thunderstorms in the afternoon.

The monastery was built on a slope, and water always gathered on one side during heavy rain.

"Please change the wall panels at the bottom!" Master instructed Little Monk. "They have been soaking for too long, and they are rotting!"

Sure enough, the panels close to the ground fell off as soon as Little Monk tugged on them. Master brought over new wood panels. He and Little Monk worked on reconstructing the wall.

随遇随喜
YIELD TO JOY

小沙弥一面钉一面指着旁边的松树问："这是松，那也是松，这也泡水，那也泡水，为什么松树不烂？"

"活着不烂，死了才烂。"

秋天，禅院里的樱花树突然枯了，裂开的树皮里爬出好多白蚁。

"怪了！春天不是还开花吗？"小沙弥说。

As he hammered the panels, Little Monk pointed to a nearby pine tree and said, "This is pine, and that is pine too. This soaked in water, and that soaked in water too. How come the pine tree did not rot?"

"Something that is alive does not rot. It will rot only after it dies."

That autumn, the monastery's cherry blossom tree suddenly withered. Many termites crawled out of the cracked bark.

"Strange! Wasn't it just blooming this spring?" observed Little Monk.

"早上还唱歌的人，不是可能中午就死了吗？"师父说，"死总等在那儿，就像白蚁，总等在这儿，树烂一点，它吃一点。你活着，它不吃；你死了，它就吃。死一寸，吃一寸。"

冬至，禅院里的树叶全掉光了，后山上也是一片寒林。傍晚，突然飘下密密的雪花。

"叶子没了，天地就宽了。树枝的手空了，上天就抛下白银。"

"Someone who was singing in the morning could be dead by noon, right?" said Master. "Death is always there, just like termites. Termites are always waiting there; when the tree rots a little, they eat a little. When the tree is alive, they don't eat; when the tree dies, they eat. If one inch dies, then one inch gets eaten."

By winter solstice, the monastery's trees had lost all their leaves. The mountains' forests were also bare. That evening, dense snowflakes suddenly fell from the sky.

"When the leaves are gone, the sky is wide open. When the branches are empty-handed, the heavens toss down silver," said Master to Little Monk.

随遇随喜
YIELD TO JOY

师父对小沙弥说："看看那山上的树，光秃秃的枝子，一个样儿，可是里面有多少死、多少生？多少看来死了，却偷偷生根；多少看来活着，却偷偷烂了。你能不警惕，不精进吗？"

"警惕精进什么？"小沙弥不懂。

"想想蛀虫是不是等在旁边！想想自己是不是正在腐烂？想想身边的水是不是已经臭了？想想还能不能保有慧根！"

"Look at those trees on the mountain. Their bare branches all look the same, but among them, how many are dead and how many are alive? Some branches look dead, but they are secretly taking root. Some look alive, but they are secretly rotting. How can you not stay alert and constantly improve?"

"Alert about what? Improve on what?" Little Monk was confused.

"Think about whether termites are waiting nearby! Think: are you gradually rotting? Think: is your surrounding water stinking? Think about whether you can grow and preserve roots of wisdom!"

随时、随性、随遇、随缘、随喜

Yield

三伏天，禅院中的草地枯
黄了一大片。

"快撒点草种子吧！好难
看哪！"小沙弥说。

"等天凉了。"师父挥挥手，
"随时！"

中秋，师父买了一包草籽，
叫小沙弥去播种。

秋风起，草籽边撒边飘。

On the hottest day of the year,
the monastery's grass was largely
dry and yellow.

"Let's hurry and plant some grass
seeds! This looks awful!" Little
Monk said.

"Wait until the days are cooler,"
Master said, waving his hand.
"Yield to time!"

Later in mid-autumn, Master
bought a package of grass seeds
and asked Little Monk to plant
them.

In the autumn wind, grass seeds
flew around as they were being
planted.

"不好了！好多种子都被吹飞了。"小沙弥喊。

"没关系，吹走的多半是空的，撒下去也发不了芽。"师父说，"随性！"

撒完种子，跟着就飞来几只小鸟啄食。

"要命了！种子都被鸟吃了！"小沙弥急得跳脚。

"Oh no! So many seeds have been blown away!" shouted Little Monk.

"Don't worry. Most of the seeds that blew away were empty. They would not sprout, even if they stayed on the ground," said Master. "Yield to nature!"

As soon as the seeds were all planted, a few birds flew over to eat.

"This is terrible! The birds will eat all the seeds!" Little Monk was jumping with frustration.

随遇随喜
YIELD TO JOY

"没关系！种子多，吃不完！"师父说，"随遇！"

半夜一阵骤雨，小沙弥早晨冲进禅房：

"师父！这下真完了！好多草籽被雨冲走了！"

"冲到哪儿，就在哪儿发！"师父说，"随缘！"

"Don't worry! There are too many seeds for the birds to eat them all," said Master. "Yield to the situation!"

There was heavy rainfall overnight. Little Monk rushed into his Master's room in the morning and shouted, "Master! It's really over now! So many seeds were washed away by the rain!"

"Wherever the seeds wash away to, they will sprout there!" said Master. "Yield to destiny!"

随遇随喜
YIELD TO JOY

一个多星期过去。

原本光秃的地面，居然长出许多青翠的草苗。一些原来没播种的角落，也泛出了绿意。

小沙弥高兴得直拍手。

师父点点头："随喜！"

More than a week passed.

Many fresh green sprouts of grass grew out of the previously bare ground. Some corners where no seeds had been planted also turned green.

Little Monk clapped with happiness.

Master nodded and said, "Yield to joy!"

点一炉好火

Light a Good Fire

不知是不是因为地球暖化，二月初，突然暖得跟春天似的，原先满地的白雪全融化了。

"快去捡柴！"师父对小沙弥说。

"天这么暖，还要点暖炉吗？"小沙弥问。

"不趁天暖雪融，落在地上的枯枝露出来，难道要等再下一场雪，到雪里挖？"

Perhaps due to global climate change, in early February, it was suddenly as warm as spring. All the snow that was covering the ground melted away.

"Hurry and go collect firewood!" Master said to Little Monk.

"It is so warm. Do we still have to light the hearth?" Little Monk asked.

"If you do not grasp the opportunity of melted snow revealing the branches on the ground, then are you going to wait until the next snowstorm and dig for branches in the snow?"

师父瞪小沙弥一眼："天暖的时候存柴，天寒的时候烧柴；好光景存粮，坏年头吃粮，你怎么连这都不懂？"

果然没过两天，又降到冰点以下。师父带着小沙弥，先把旧报纸揉成一团团堆在壁炉下面，放上小树枝，再从柴房抱来大木柴，搁在顶上。

Master glared at Little Monk. "Store firewood when the weather is warm; burn firewood when the weather is cold. Store grain when it is a plentiful year; eat grain when it is a bad year. How do you not even know this?"

Two days later, the temperature dropped below freezing. Master taught Little Monk to first crumple up old newspapers and pile them under the fireplace, add the small branches, and then bring the big logs in from storage to place on top.

随遇随喜
YIELD TO JOY

师父划根火柴，把下面的报纸点着，延烧到小枯枝，发出噼啪声，接着腾起熊熊的火焰，还不时夹着火星，像烟花盛会似的在炉子里飞窜。

小沙弥兴奋地直拍手叫好。

"叫什么好？"师父推推小沙弥，"快把炉门关小！"

火苗一下子收敛了，小沙弥看看师父："会熄的！"

Master lit a match and transferred the flame to the newspaper. Then, the fire reached the small branches, causing crackling sounds. Next, it turned into blazing flames with sparks, flying and dancing like fireworks.

Little Monk excitedly clapped his hands and cheered.

"What are you cheering for?" Master nudged Little Monk. "Hurry and close the fireplace door!"

The flames suddenly weakened. Little Monk looked at Master and said, "The fire will go out!"

随遇随喜
YIELD TO JOY

"熄不了！反而会烧得更好。"师父笑道，"火就像人间的爱情，那爱得死去活来，好像一刻也分不开的热恋，常常来得疾也去得快。

"It won't go out! In fact, it will be an even better fire."

Master laughed. "Fire is just like humans' love. The kind of passionate and inseparable love that is like life and death often comes quickly but also goes away quickly.

"不信你下次不关炉门，看那大火能烧多久，只怕上面的柴还没热，炉子已经冷却。反不如把炉门关小，让下面的火慢慢烧，把大块的柴先烧透。"

果然，大木块的边缘渐渐冒烟，露出火苗。

"着是着了，但是火不大耶！"小沙弥说。

"不要大，要稳！夜里够暖就成了。"

If you don't believe me, next time, don't close the fireplace door, and see how long that blazing fire can last. Before the logs on top even get hot, the hearth will already be cold. Instead, we are closing the fireplace door and letting the fire slowly burn from below, until the large logs are thoroughly burnt."

Sure enough, the edges of the large logs gradually emitted smoke and then sparks.

"The logs are on fire, but it's not a big fire!" said Little Monk.

"We don't want big; we want steady! It just needs to keep us warm throughout the night."

随遇随喜
YIELD TO JOY

但是天没亮，小沙弥就被冻醒。爬过去看火炉，只见几块黑炭，散在炉子四处。"不得了了！师父！是谁把柴动过，火都熄了。"

师父张开眼睛，看一眼："少见多怪！那些大块的柴，愈烧愈小，当然显得愈来愈远。跟人一样，愈久愈远，愈远愈淡。你快用火钳，把小炭块拢到一起！"

However, before sunrise, Little Monk was woken up by the cold. He crawled over to the fireplace, and all he saw were a few pieces of char, scattered around the hearth. "Oh no! Master! Someone moved the wood, and now the fire is out."

Master opened his eyes and took one look. "Everything is strange to those who haven't seen much! Large logs become smaller as they burn, and therefore they seem farther and farther apart. They are just like humans who are physically apart and feel emotionally distant over time. Quickly take the fire tongs and move the small pieces of char together!"

小沙弥照办了，看似已经熄灭的黑炭，聚成一堆，居然很快地变红，接着蹿出火苗。

"死灰复燃了！死灰复燃了！"小沙弥喊。

"胡说！死了怎么复燃？就因为没死，所以复燃；就因为重聚，所以重温。快睡吧！"

Little Monk did as he was told. When the black char was gathered into a pile, the pieces quickly turned red, and then flames appeared.

"The dead ash is rekindled! The dead ash is rekindled!" Little Monk shouted.

"Nonsense! How can something that's dead be rekindled? It can only be rekindled because it never died. Reunion brings back warmth. Go to sleep!"

随遇随喜
YIELD TO JOY

小沙弥醒来，天已经大亮，窗上结了一层冰，禅房里却挺温暖。原来师父又添了几块柴，壁炉里一片蕴藉。

"今天的火更棒了！"小沙弥说。

"今天的火不是昨天的火吗？"师父说，"今天的火不是从昨天来的吗？柴变了，火没变。"

Little Monk woke up. The sky was already bright, and a layer of ice had formed on the window. But inside the room, it was warm. Apparently, Master had added more firewood, and the fireplace was full of steady heat.

"Today's fire is even better!" Little Monk said.

"Is today's fire not yesterday's fire?" said Master. "Didn't today's fire come from yesterday's fire? It is different wood, but it is the same fire."

小和尚伸个懒腰，趴着窗子往外看，接着大叫："外面好冷啊！连小鸟都变不见了。雪好深哪！连墙都变矮了。"

师父走到窗前看了看，扶着小沙弥的肩膀："小鸟真没了吗？墙真矮了吗？这世界真变了吗？景气不同，世界没变。谁不知道冬天过去就是春天？你还怕春天不来吗？"

Little Monk stretched and looked out the window. He shouted, "It's so cold outside! Even the birds have disappeared. The snow is so deep! Even the wall became shorter."

Master walked to the window, held Little Monk's shoulders, and said, "Did the birds really disappear? Did the wall really become shorter? Has this world changed? The scenery is different, but it is the same world. Who doesn't know that after winter passes, spring comes? How can you fear that spring won't come?"

随遇随喜
YIELD TO JOY

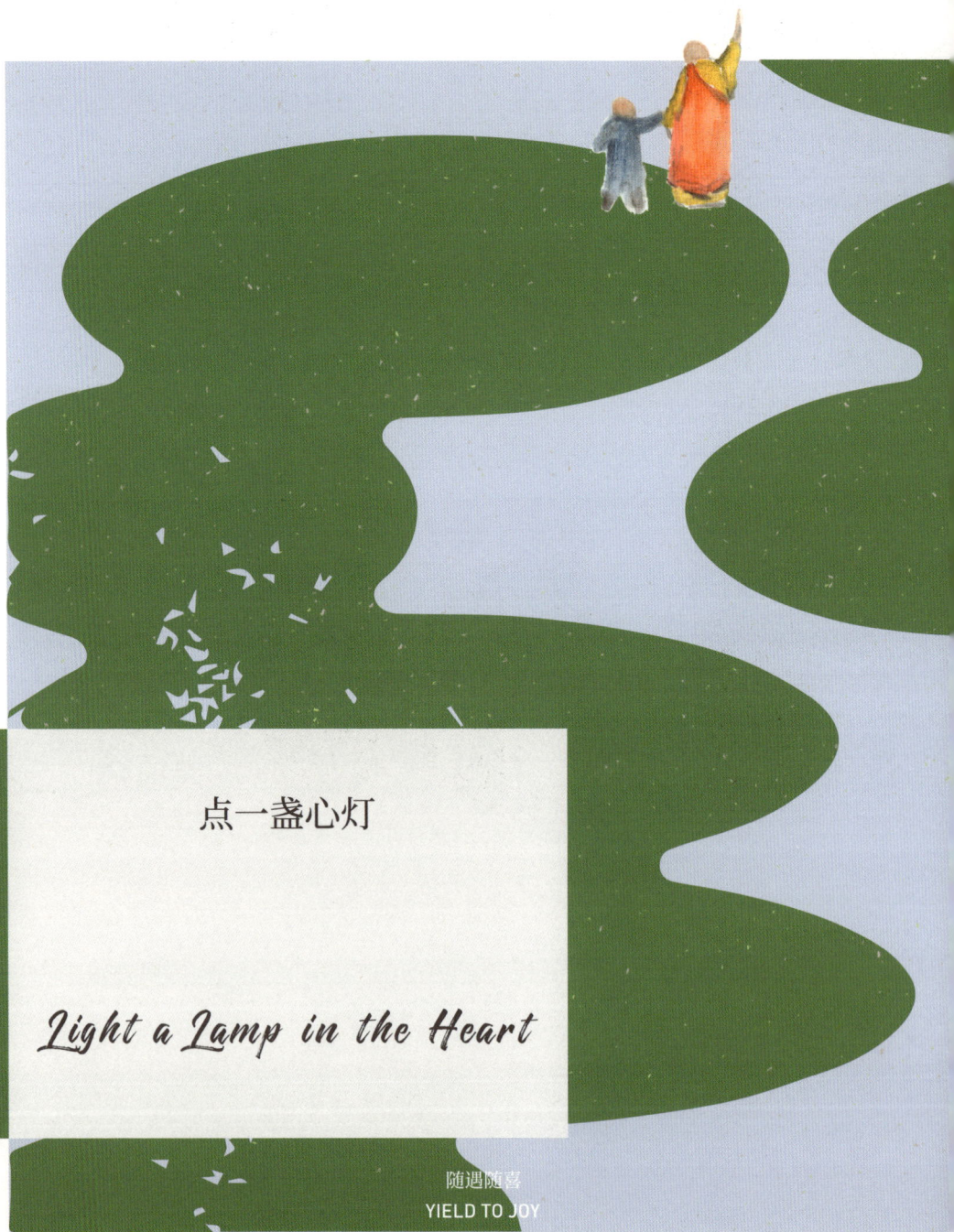

点一盏心灯

Light a Lamp in the Heart

小沙弥去见师父："师父！我遁入空门已经多年，每天在这青山白云之间，茹素礼佛、暮鼓晨钟，经读得愈多，心中的杂念不但不减，反而增加，怎么办？"

"点一盏灯，使它非但能照亮你，而且不会留下你的身影，就可以悟了！"

Little Monk went to see Master and said, "Master! I have already been in the monastery for many years. Every day, I live among the mountains and clouds, obey a vegetarian diet, and follow the morning clock and evening drum rituals. But no matter how much I read scripture, the chaotic thoughts in my heart are not diminishing but rather increasing. What should I do?"

"Light a lamp. Let it illuminate you, yet not make a shadow. Then you will understand!"

数十年过去······

有一座禅院远近驰名，大家都称之为"万灯院"，因为其中点满了灯，成千上万的灯，使人走入其间，仿佛步入一片灯海，灿烂辉煌。

Decades later...

There was a very famous temple, which everyone called The Temple of Ten Thousand Lamps because it was full of brightly lit lamps. When people walked in, they felt like they were entering a sea of light — brilliant and glorious.

这所万灯院的住持，就是当年的小沙弥。虽然如今年事已高，并拥有上千的徒众，但是他仍然不快乐。因为尽管他每做一桩功德，都点一盏灯，却无论把灯放在脚边、悬在顶上，乃至以一片灯海将自己团团围住，还是总会见到自己的影子。甚至可以说，灯愈亮，影子愈显；灯愈多，影子也愈多。

This temple's abbot was the Little Monk from years ago. Although he was now of old age and had over a thousand disciples, he was still not happy. Every time he performed an act of kindness, he lit a lamp. But regardless of whether he placed the lamp at his feet or above his head, or even when he was surrounded by a sea of lamps, he could still see his own shadow. One could say that the brighter the lamp, the clearer the shadow; the more lamps there were, the more shadows there were.

他困惑了，却已经没有师父可以问，因为师父早已死去，自己也将不久人世。

他圆寂了，据说就在死前终于通悟。

他没有在万灯之间找到一生寻求的东西，却在黑暗的禅房里通悟：身外的成就再高，灯再亮，却只能造成身后的影子。唯有一个方法，能使自己皎然澄澈，心无挂碍。

他点了一盏心灯！

He was confused, but there was no more master to ask, as his Master had died long ago. He himself would leave this world soon too.

He passed away. Supposedly right before his death, he finally understood.

He did not find what he was looking for his whole life among the ten thousand lamps, but he found it in his dark meditation room. He realized that even the greatest external accomplishments and the brightest lamps would only result in shadows. There was only one solution: purifying his soul, clearing his heart of all distractions.

He lit a lamp in his heart!

随遇随喜
YIELD TO JOY

著作权合同登记号：图字 18-2020-106

图书在版编目（CIP）数据

随遇随喜：刘墉写给大家的生活禅：汉、英 / 刘墉绘著；刘轩，刘倚帆译 . -- 长沙：湖南文艺出版社，2020.10
ISBN 978-7-5404-9783-5

Ⅰ . ①随… Ⅱ . ①刘… ②刘… ③刘… Ⅲ . ①人生哲学—通俗读物—汉、英 Ⅳ . ① B821-49

中国版本图书馆 CIP 数据核字（2020）第 155370 号

上架建议：畅销·成功励志

SUIYU SUIXI: LIU YONG XIE GEI DAJIA DE SHENGHUOCHAN
随遇随喜：刘墉写给大家的生活禅

作　　者：刘　墉
译　　者：刘　轩　刘倚帆
出 版 人：曾赛丰
责任编辑：丁丽丹
监　　制：小博集
策划编辑：文赛峰
特约编辑：李孟思
营销支持：付　佳　余孟玲
版权支持：刘子一
封面设计：利　锐
版式设计：利　锐
出　　版：湖南文艺出版社
　　　　　（长沙市雨花区东二环一段 508 号　邮编：410014）
网　　址：www.hnwy.net
印　　刷：旺源文化发展（天津）有限公司
经　　销：新华书店
开　　本：680 mm×955 mm　　1/16
字　　数：61 千字
印　　张：9
版　　次：2020 年 10 月第 1 版
印　　次：2020 年 10 月第 1 次印刷
书　　号：ISBN 978-7-5404-9783-5
定　　价：39.80 元

若有质量问题，请致电质量监督电话：010-59096394
团购电话：010-59320018